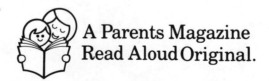

A Parents Magazine
Read Aloud Original.

But No Elephants

by Jerry Smath

Parents Magazine Press ♥ New York

To my mother,
Helen Dolechek Smath

Library of Congress Cataloging in Publication Data
Smath, Jerry.
　　But no elephants.
　　SUMMARY: Grandma Tildy finally agrees to take an
unwanted elephant into her home, but soon regrets
her decision.
　　[1. Elephants—Fiction.　2. Pets—Fiction]
I. Title
PZ7.S6393Bu　　　[E]　　　79–16136
ISBN 0–8193–1007–7
ISBN 0–8193–1008–5 lib. bdg.

Grandma Tildy lived all alone.
She worked hard every day.
She had no time to play.

One day a man came to her house.
He was selling pets.

"Would you like to buy a canary bird?"
asked the man.

"Very well," said Grandma Tildy.
"But no elephants!"

Grandma Tildy was cooking stew.
The bird wanted to help.
So he sang a song for her.

It made Grandma Tildy happy.

That night they sat down to eat
the stew together.

And it tasted better than ever before.

The next day the pet man came again.
"Would you like to buy a beaver?"
he asked.

"Very well," said Grandma Tildy.
"But no elephants!"

Grandma Tildy needed firewood.
The beaver wanted to help.
So he cut the wood with his
sharp teeth.

That night they sat in front of
a warm fire.

Grandma Tildy went shopping.
She met the pet man again.

"Would you like to buy a turtle?"
he asked.

"Very well," she said.
"But no elephants!"

Grandma Tildy was tired.
The turtle wanted to help.
So he carried her home on his back.

That night Grandma Tildy washed the turtle and put him to bed.

The next day it rained hard.
The roof started to leak.

Then someone knocked on the door.
It was you-know-who.

"Would you like to buy a woodpecker?"
the pet man asked.

"Very well," said Grandma Tildy.
"But no elephants!"

The woodpecker wanted to help.
So he nailed the roof down tight.
The dripping stopped.

That night they all danced together in the warm, dry house.

The days got colder and colder.
Grandma Tildy put food in jars
for the winter.

"I don't like the cold," she said.
Just then the pet man appeared.

"Would you like to buy an elephant?"
he asked.
"He's the only animal left,
and I must leave before it snows."

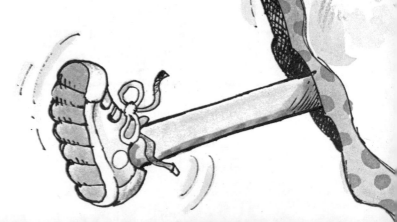

"No! No elephants!" shouted Grandma.
She went back to her work.
The pet man left.

But the elephant stayed.
It started to snow.
And it kept on snowing . . .

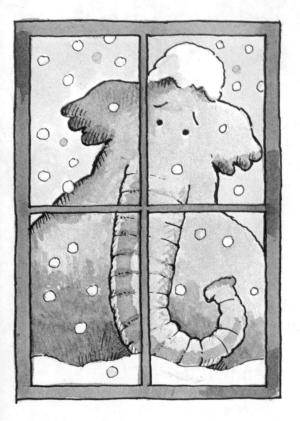

and snowing . . .

and snowing . . .

and snowing.

"No elephants!" said Grandma Tildy.
But the elephant would not go.

They could not see the elephant now.
But they could hear him crying.
They felt sad.

"Very well," called Grandma Tildy.
"You may come in."
The elephant was as happy as could be.

But the elephant had a problem.
He could not get through the door.

So they all helped to push him inside.

"Oh, dear," said Grandma Tildy.
"I hope the floor is strong.
This is a very old house."

Outside, the snow kept falling.
But inside the house it was cozy and warm.
Everyone hoped winter would go away
and spring would come soon.

That night there was a terrible crash.

The elephant had fallen
through the floor.

"We cannot fix this," said Grandma.
"You will just have to stay there."

The winter was long.
And soon the firewood was gone.
The elephant was always hungry.
He kept eating . . .

and eating . . .

and eating . . .
until all the food was gone.

"We cannot leave or we will freeze,"
said Grandma Tildy.

"We cannot stay or we will starve.
What are we to do?"

The elephant felt sorry.
Then he thought of a way to help.

He started to walk.

He walked and walked . . .

and walked and walked.

When he stopped, they were in
a warm, sunny place.

And that is where Grandma Tildy
and her friends are today.